Big Heli and Little Heli

Written by Jill Eggleton
Illustrated by Simon Bosch

SPLASH

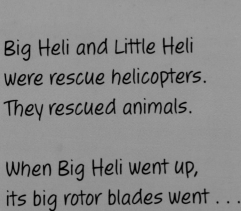

Big Heli and Little Heli
were rescue helicopters.
They rescued animals.

When Big Heli went up,
its big rotor blades went . . .

thrump, thrump, thrump!

But when Little Heli went up,
its little rotor blades went . . .

meeeeeeeeeeee,

and it buzzed through the sky
like a bumblebee!

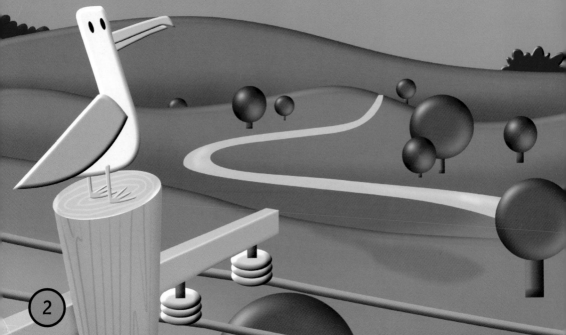

Big Heli and Little Heli waited
on the helicopter pad.
A radio voice said,
"Helicopters, helicopters, hurry, hurry, hurry!"

Up went Big Heli.

Thrump, thrump, thrump!

Up went Little Heli,

meeeeeeeeeeee,

buzz, buzz, buzzing like a bumblebee!

Big Heli and Little Heli flew over houses.
They flew over the city and all the way
to the beach.
And there – on the beach –
was a big blue whale.
It was stuck in the sand,
and it couldn't get back in the water.

Down went Big Heli's winch . . .

down, down, down.

The people on the beach
put a net over the whale,
and they hooked it up
to Big Heli's winch.

Up went Big Heli.
Its big rotor blades went . . .

thrump, thrump, thrump!

It took the whale out to sea
and plopped it back in the water.

The people on the beach clapped and shouted,
"Hooray for Big Heli."

But Little Heli didn't do anything, anything at all.
Little Heli was far too small.

Big Heli and Little Heli went back
to the helicopter pad and waited.
Then the radio voice said,
"Helicopters, helicopters, hurry, hurry, hurry!"

Up went Big Heli.

Thrump, thrump, thrump!

Up went Little Heli,

meeeeeeeeee,

buzz, buzz, buzzing
like a bumblebee!

Big Heli and Little Heli
flew over houses.
They flew over the city,
and all the way to the jungle.
And there was an elephant
lying in the grass.
The elephant had a sore leg,
and it couldn't walk.

Down went Big Heli's winch . . .

down, down, down.

The people in the jungle
put an enormous net
around the elephant,
and they hooked it up
to Big Heli's winch.

Up went Big Heli,

thrump, thrump, thrump!

Big Heli took the elephant
to the animal hospital.

But Little Heli didn't
do anything, anything at all.
Little Heli was far too small.

One day, Big Heli and Little Heli were
called all the way to the mountains.

Way down,
between two rocky walls,
was a baby eagle bird.
It had fallen out of its nest,
and it couldn't fly.

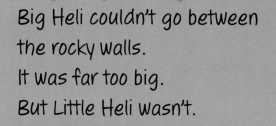

Big Heli couldn't go between
the rocky walls.
It was far too big.
But Little Heli wasn't.

So, down went Little Heli,
very, very slowly.
It was a dangerous job,
and Little Heli had to be very careful.

When Little Heli was close enough,
it picked up the baby eagle
in a scoop like a giant spoon,
and took it back to its mother
in the nest.

Why couldn't
Big Heli
do anything?

The people on the mountain
clapped and shouted,
"Hooray for Little Heli."

But Big Heli couldn't do anything,
anything at all.

Sometimes, you need to be small.

Song

Up went Big Heli . . .
up, up, up.
Its big rotor blades went . . .

thrump, thrump, thrump!

Up went Little Heli . . .

Meeeeee,

buzzing through the sky
like a bumblebee.

Meeeeeeeeeeee!

Buzz, buzz, buzzing
like a bumblebee.

Storyboard

1

2

5

6

Letter Play

Which words start the same as buzz?

Helpful Hint: Read the Splash speech bubble. Say: buzz starts with a b. Which words start the same as buzz?

monkey

boat

helicopter

bird

Books Available in the Splash Series

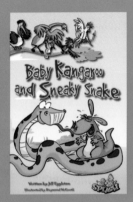

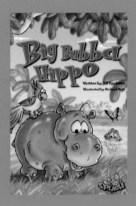

Crocodile in the Jungle River

The Jelly Bean Tree

The Little Yellow Car

Where Is the Sun?

Bird Cat

Ariel and Poppy Woppy

The Big Buzzy Honey Bun

Granny McQueen and the Popcorn Machine

Butterfly Magic

Fire Dog Frizzle

Mucky-Yucky Eaters

Digby the Digger Dog

About the Author

Jill Eggleton is a prolific author and educational consultant who has worked in the international literacy arena for more than twenty years, and as a classroom teacher for thirty. She is coauthor of the acclaimed **Sails Literacy Series**, a comprehensive literacy reading program.

Reading to Children

This story is for reading to your child or a group of children.

The foundations of learning to read are set down from the moment a child first hears the sounds of people talking, the tunes of songs, and the rhythm and sounds of language in rhymes and stories. Reading aloud to children early in life also develops their speaking skills quickly. Having conversations about books helps children to develop thinking skills. And reading aloud and talking about what you are reading helps children to develop concentration skills and the ability to solve problems.

Reading aloud to children exposes them to words. Children will learn to love words, and when they love words, they will use them in their own speaking and writing. When children hear words over and over, they become familiar, and familiar words are always easier to add into their vocabulary bank than unfamiliar words.

Reading aloud every day will help your child or children to **comprehend stories**. It will help to increase **vocabulary**. It will let children hear the flow of language, and they will learn about **fluency**. It will provide the foundations for **phonemic awareness** and **phonic knowledge**. Phonics is essential in learning to read, and children who can identify the letters of the alphabet before school meet early success as readers.

However, the **"stories first"** approach is the key to creating the desire in children to participate in the world of literacy. Children who have been entertained by wonderful stories have a joyful attitude toward learning to read. If you read aloud to children on a daily basis, they will soon begin to understand the look of print, the way words work in sentences, and how the world works – they will begin to see why this happens and that happens, and how it all comes together to mean something.

In other words, they learn to read.